STRONG
to the
HOOP

by **John Coy**

illustrations by
Leslie Jean-Bart

LEE & LOW BOOKS, INC. • New York

Special thanks to the students of Saturn/River Front and the Loft. —J.C.

Text copyright © 1999 by John Coy
Illustrations copyright © 1999 by Leslie Jean-Bart

LEE & LOW BOOKS Inc., 95 Madison Avenue, New York, NY 10016
leeandlow.com

Manufactured in China by RR Donnelley

Book Design by Christy Hale
Book Production by The Kids at Our House

The text is set in Blur Light
The collage illustrations are rendered using photography and scratchboard drawings.
Polaroid transfers are then made from the collages to create the final images.

(HC) 15 14 13 12 11 10 9 8 7 6
(PB) 20 19 18 17 16

Library of Congress Cataloging-in-Publication Data
Coy, John.
Strong to the hoop / by John Coy ; illustrations by Leslie Jean-Bart. — 1st ed.
p.   cm.
Summary: Ten-year-old James tries to hold his own and prove himself on the
basketball court when the older boys finally ask him to join them in a game.
ISBN-13: 978-1-880000-80-9 (hardcover)   ISBN-13: 978-1-58430-178-3 (paperback)
[1. Basketball—Fiction.]   I. Jean-Bart, Leslie, ill.   II. Title.
PZ7.C839457St   1999
[Fic]—DC21   98-33264   CIP AC

MIX
Paper from
responsible sources
FSC® C144853
www.fsc.org

For Fiona and Sophie—J.C.

To my mother and to "Turk"—L.J.-B.

Wump, wump, wump.
The ball bounces as my big brother Nate and I walk into the park.

At the court everybody shakes hands, and the guys split into two teams of four, Shirts and Skins. I wish I was big enough to play, but because I'm only ten I go to the side court.

No other kids are here, so I practice my game. I dribble, aim for the hoop, shoot, get the ball, shoot, over and over.

Back on the main court, Zo glides down the lane, fakes a pass, then flips a finger roll with his left hand. So smooth, it looks like slow motion.

Now I imagine playing as an All-Star.

Tie game, nine seconds left.

I bounce the ball with my left hand. No one's open.

Six, five, four.

I drive left, spin right, and soar to the hoop. Ehnn! The buzzer sounds.

"Oh no," Luke yells. He lies under the basket grabbing his ankle. "I'm done. You need another player."

"How about James?" Slinky points to me.
"You want to run?"

"Yeah!" I race onto the court.

Nate and the guys gather round me.

"He's not big enough," says Marcus.
"Someone else will show."

"We're not waiting." Zo picks up the ball.
"C'mon James, you're a Skin."

I peel off my shirt and think how skinny my body looks.

"You guard Marcus," says Nate. "Stick to him."

I look up at Marcus who's a head taller. His muscles push out his shirt.

Maybe I'm not ready to be out here.

"Three, three. Game's fifteen."

Right away the ball goes to Marcus. I slip and fall to the asphalt as he goes to the hoop.

Out of nowhere, Slinky leaps to block the shot. "Get that out of here."

"Slide your feet," Nate tells me.

Slinky nods and flips a pass. I feel the worn leather, bounce it twice, and pass to Zo.

"Count it," he says as the ball leaves his hand.

Someday I want to be able to shoot like that.

"Play back on Marcus," Nate says. "Make him shoot outside."

I move back, bending my knees and shuffling my feet.

Marcus bounces the ball and looks right at me. "You can't guard me." His shot rattles off the rim. Zo rebounds, and we race the other way.

I cut through the lane and bump
into Marcus. It's like running into a
rock.

"You're too small. Get out of
here or I'll push you out."

I don't like his talking. Why can't
he just shut up and play?

At midcourt, Zo swats a loose ball and I have a wide open lay-up. Shoot it softly, I remind myself.

"Miss," Marcus yells from behind, and the ball bangs off the rim.

I feel everyone's eyes on me and want to crawl off the court.

"Go strong to the hoop," says Nate.

"We gotta have those," says Zo.

I know. I shouldn't be out here if I miss a shot like that.

Up and down we go. I bang against legs and hips to stay with Marcus. An elbow hits my head, but I keep my feet. I'm breathing so hard my lungs feel on fire, and my mouth is so dry I can't spit.

I dive for a ball that's going out of
bounds and make the save.

"You okay?" Nate asks.

I feel the burn on my knee and
see blood, but I know what to say.

"Yeah, I'm fine." We
sprint down court.

Marcus makes a move and I grab him.

Trchh.

"What are you doing?" he yells. "You ripped my shirt."

"Call the foul then." I'm sorry about the shirt but sick of his talking.

"Foul. And keep your hands off me."

I see the guys watching and I'm surprised to hear my voice.

"Then keep your hands off me at the other end."

"What? I don't need to hold you." Marcus says.

"Okay you two," Slinky says. "Let's play ball."

A crowd has gathered around the court and someone's turned on music.

"Finish it off, Marcus," a tall kid shouts. "We've got winners."

Marcus leans forward and makes a move. I slide my feet and the ball hits his leg and skips out of bounds. He glares at me but doesn't say a thing.

I zoom down court, ferocious like a lion. I bounce pass to Slinky, who scores off the board.

"Nice look." He hits my hand.

"The kid can hoop," a man in dark glasses says as I hurry back on defense.

"Okay kid," Marcus sneers. "You and me." He pushes off me and hits a jumper.

My legs feel heavy now as the sun bakes the asphalt.

"Fourteen, fourteen. Game point." Zo bounces the ball like a yo-yo between his legs. "This is it."

The team that wins keeps playing and I feel my heart beating. I wipe my hands on my shorts, but right away they're sweaty again.

Zo zips a pass to Nate. I bump my shoulder against Marcus. Nate passes back to Zo, and Marcus rushes to double team. Zo passes to me.

"Shoot it."

I turn and shoot in one smooth motion.

"Yes!" yells Nate. "Game point by James." He and Slinky lift me up and I grin a championship smile.

"That was our plan," says Zo. "Go to James for the game. You guys couldn't stop him."

"Good game, James." Marcus slaps my hand.

"Good game, Marcus." I'm happy as the last day of school.

At the hoop, four new players are warming up.

"You need one?" someone shouts.

"No," says Nate. "We've got our four."

I can't believe I'm on the main court with these guys. I feel strong enough to run all afternoon.

"Zero, zero. Going to fifteen," I call. "Ball's in."